MW00880278

Hello Big Red!

Aimee Aryal

Illustrated by Megan Craig

MASCOT BOOKS
www.mascotbooks.com

It was a beautiful fall day at the
University of Arkansas.

Big Red was on his way to
Razorback Stadium to watch
a football game.

He walked by Mullins Library.

A professor walking by said,
"Hello Big Red!"

Big Red passed by the
Greek Theatre.

A girl studying there waved,
"Hello Big Red!"

Big Red went over to
Bud Walton Arena where the
Razorbacks play basketball.

An Arkansas fan standing outside said,
"Hello Big Red!"

Big Red passed by the Arkansas Union.

Some students walking nearby
shouted, "Hello Big Red!"

It was almost time for the football game.
As Big Red walked to the stadium,
he passed by some alumni.

The alumni remembered Big Red from when they went to Arkansas. They said, "Hello, again, Big Red!"

Finally, Big Red arrived at
Razorback Stadium.

As he ran onto the football field,
the crowd called,
"Wooo. Pig. Sooie! Go Hogs!"

Big Red watched the game
from the sidelines and
cheered for the team.

The Razorbacks scored six points!
The quarterback shouted,
"Touchdown Big Red!"

At half-time the
Razorback Marching Band
performed on the field.

Big Red and the crowd sang the "University of Arkansas Fight Song."

The Arkansas Razorbacks
won the football game!

Big Red gave Coach Nutt a high-five.
The coach said,
"Great game Big Red!"

After the football game, Big Red
was tired. It had been a long day at
the University of Arkansas.

He walked home and climbed into bed.

"Goodnight Big Red."

For Anna and Maya,
and all of Big Red's little fans. ~ AA

Dedicated in loving memory of Patti, who would have been
very appreciative and supportive of this book. ~ MC

Special thanks to:

Houston Nutt

Matt Shanklin

Copyright © 2004 by Mascot Books, Inc. All rights reserved.
No part of this book may be reproduced by any means.

For information please contact Mascot Books,
P.O. Box 220157, Chantilly, VA 20153-0157.

ARKANSAS RAZORBACKS, UNIVERSITY OF ARKANSAS, ARKANSAS, RAZORBACKS, RAZORBACK,
GO HOGS, WOOO PIG SOOIE are trademarks or registered trademarks of the
University of Arkansas and are used under license.

ISBN: 1-932888-24-1

Printed in the United States.

www.mascotbooks.com